The Power of
Henry's Imagination

The Power of
Henry's Imagination

story by
SKYE BYRNE & NIC GEORGE
pictures by

ALADDIN

New York   London   Toronto   Sydney   New Delhi

ALADDIN

An imprint of Simon & Schuster
Children's Publishing Division • 1230 Avenue
of the Americas, New York, New York 10020 • First
Aladdin hardcover edition October 2015 • Copyright © 2015
by Cuppa Cooish LLC. • Background landscape photographs
copyright © 2015 by Thinkstock • Star chart copyright © 2015 by
Larry McNish • All rights reserved, including the right of reproduction
in whole or in part in any form. • ALADDIN is a trademark of Simon &
Schuster, Inc., and related logo is a registered trademark of Simon &
Schuster, Inc. • THE SECRET text mark and THE SECRET logo are
registered trademarks of Creste LLC. • For information about special discounts
for bulk purchases, please contact Simon & Schuster Special Sales at 1-866-506-1949
or business@simonandschuster.com. • The Simon & Schuster Speakers Bureau can
bring authors to your live event. For more information or to book an event
contact the Simon & Schuster Speakers Bureau at 1-866-248-3049 or visit
our website at www.simonspeakers.com. • Designed by Dan Potash and
Nic George • The illustrations for this book were rendered in mixed media
• The text of this book was set in 1790 Royal Printing. • Manufactured
in China 0815 SCP • 10 9 8 7 6 5 4 3 2 1
• Library of Congress Control Number 2015935744 •
ISBN 978-1-4814-0626-0 (hc) •
ISBN 978-1-4814-0627-7 (eBook)

For Savannah, and for my parents,
who always allowed me to be me
—S. B.

For my Mum, Janet Hazel George,
who asked me to use my imagination
—N. G.

Henry's favorite toy was a rabbit called Raspberry.
Raspberry was white with floppy silver ears and a red
nose that looked just like a raspberry. Sometimes Henry
was sure that Raspberry smelled like raspberries too.

Henry and Raspberry had been together a very, very long time — five years, three months, and eleven and a half days, to be exact. Grandpa had given Raspberry to Henry the day Henry was born, knowing they would have many adventures.

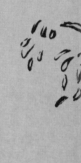

Everyone could see how much
Henry loved Raspberry.

From dawn until dusk, they did everything together.

One morning Henry decided to take Raspberry to the veggie patch to teach him how to dig up carrots. But Henry couldn't find Raspberry.

Henry looked for Raspberry in all the usual places,
like underneath Grandpa, on top of the lamp, and
inside pillowcases.

But Raspberry wasn't anywhere.

Then Henry turned his whole bedroom upside down.
But even that did not unearth Raspberry.

Henry was starting to feel worried.

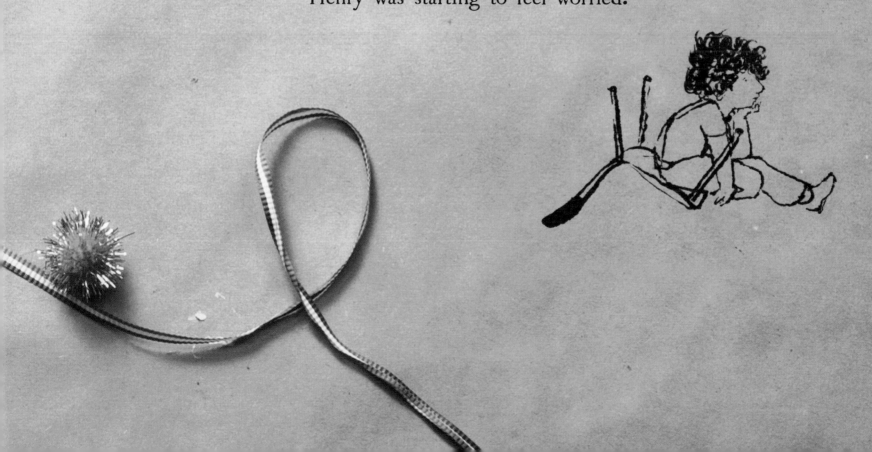

Henry got his mom and dad to help him search the whole house for Raspberry. By the time they finished, the place was a huge mess!

And they still hadn't found Raspberry.

With tears sliding down his cheeks, Henry went to
Grandpa, who was sitting in his favorite armchair,
reading one of his favorite books.

"Grandpa, can you please help me find Raspberry?
I've looked everywhere!"

Grandpa put down his book, pushed his glasses down his
nose, and leaned forward. "Henry," Grandpa said in his
warm, knowledgeable voice. "If you've looked everywhere,
then there is only one thing left to do . . ."

"You must imagine that you have Raspberry back!"

"Imagine I have Raspberry back?" Henry repeated, wiping away a tear with the back of his hand.

"Yes, Henry. It's very simple. You just have to imagine
that Raspberry is with you — in this moment!"

Then Grandpa sat down and started reading his book again. He didn't say another word. Since Grandpa knew more than anyone else who had ever lived, Henry decided the best thing to do was follow his advice.

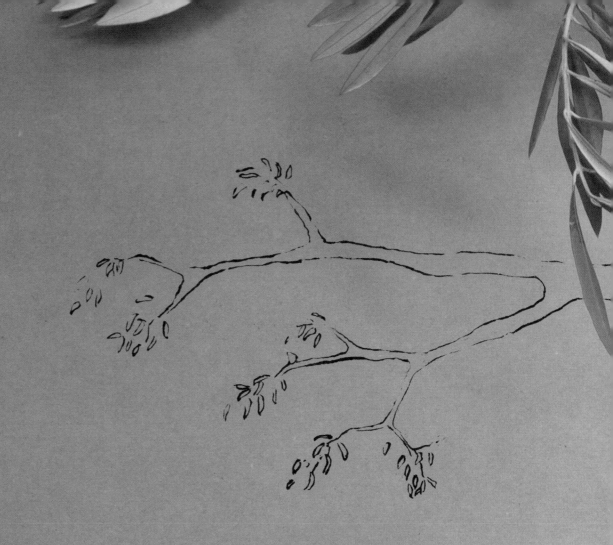

And so Henry began to imagine . . .

When Mom called him for lunch, Henry imagined that he and Raspberry were explorers climbing a mountain. They got caught in a terrible storm, and found shelter in a cave! Raspberry had to cook a can of beans for them to eat.

When Dad sent him outside to play, Henry
imagined that he and Raspberry were pirates on
a ship full of rare treasures, steering their cargo
through the crocodile-filled sea.

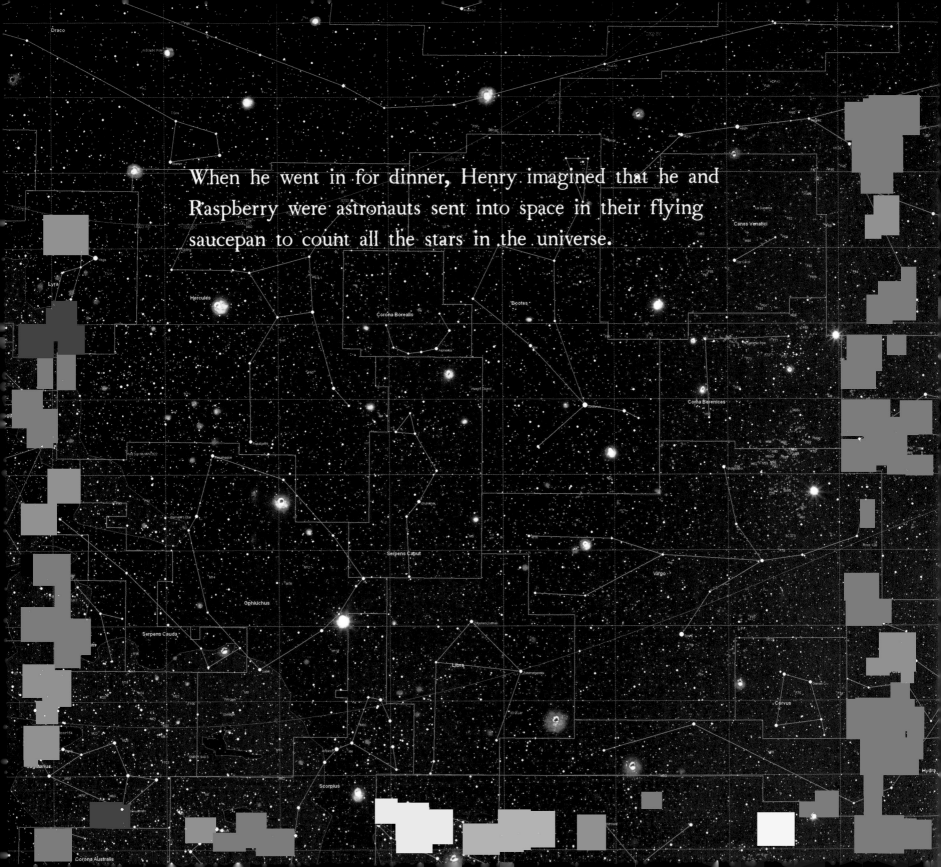

When he went in for dinner, Henry imagined that he and Raspberry were astronauts sent into space in their flying saucepan to count all the stars in the universe.

When he went to get ready for bed that night,
Henry imagined that he and Raspberry were
dragon catchers walking silently through the forest
as they searched for the mysterious purple dragon.

Henry had so much fun imagining his many adventures with Raspberry that he completely forgot Raspberry was lost in the real world. In fact, when Henry went to bed that night, he fell asleep as quickly as he did when Raspberry was in his arms.

Later that night, Grandpa heard a knock at the door.
It was Malcolm the mailman — and he was holding
Raspberry!

"I found him lying on the path," said Malcolm.
"I would have missed him if it weren't for his
silver ears shining in the moonlight!"

"Well, well, well . . . imagine that!" Grandpa
said with a wink.

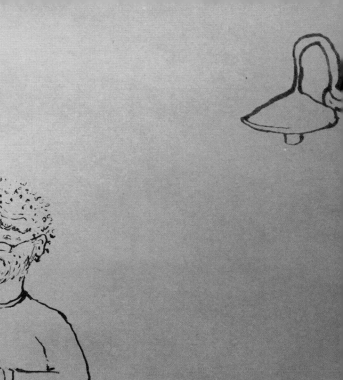

Imagine that.

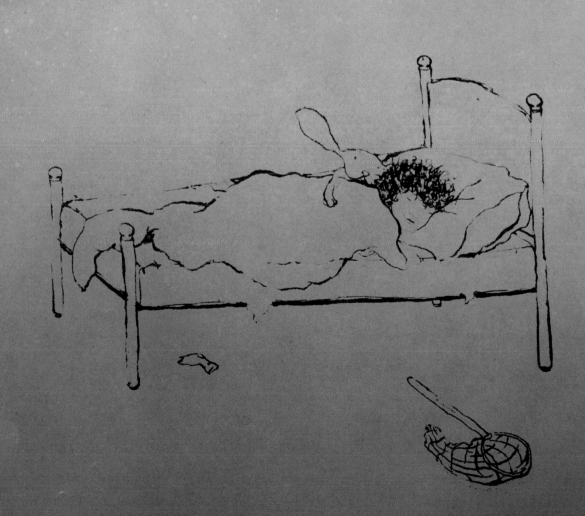